7/11 cB9 08 1 1c

Danny's Egg

COLIN THIELE
CLASSICS

Colin Thiele

Danny's Egg

Lothian
BOOKS

Thomas C. Lothian Pty Ltd
132 Albert Road, South Melbourne, Victoria 3205
www.lothian.com.au

First published by Angus & Robertson 1989
Bluegum edition published 1991
Reprinted 1991, 1992
This edition first published by
Thomas C. Lothian Pty Ltd 2002

National Library of Australia
Cataloguing-in-Publication data:

Thiele, Colin, 1920- .
Danny's egg.

For young adults.
ISBN 0 7344 0403 4.

I. Title. (Series : Colin Thiele classics).

A823.3

Cover design by Sandra Nobes
Cover and text illustrations by Robert Ingpen
Book design by Paulene Meyer
Printed in Australia by Griffin Press

Contents

1

The Emu

When Danny first saw the dark shape behind the bushes he stopped short. His heart skipped with fright. The shape had been moving about slowly but now it stood still, screened by the leaves and branches. It was big, taller than Danny himself — a thick mass below and a tapering stalk above, like a curving yacca stem. Suddenly it moved again and Danny relaxed with a smile. It was an emu.

For a moment or two they stood eyeing each other. The emu was curious. It held its head high and looked at Danny inquisitively with sharp bright eyes. Now and again it changed the angle of its gaze or moved its long neck slightly, trying to make him out. Danny grinned and peered back.

Neither of them was afraid. After a while the emu decided that Danny was not really interesting and walked out into an open patch in the scrub, picking and pecking as it went. Danny stepped from his screen of bushes and stood watching.

It was late in the afternoon. The sunlight was touching the leaves with long golden lances and the ground under the trees was speckled with shadows and shapes of sudden light. Further off, the cleared patches on the slopes of the ranges were greening with spring grass.

Danny loved the scrub lands and the ranges. His mother and father let him roam about in them as much as he liked provided he was careful and didn't go too far. He found all kinds of treasures in them: abandoned birds' nests, the bones of animals, sloughed snake skins, even old buckles and bits of harness from the old days of horsemen and drovers.

Danny moved closer to the emu, imitating its walk with long, jerky strides. He held up his arm and kinked his hand to make it look like an emu's head, pretending to be another bird following its mate. In that way they walked in line for a while until the emu stopped at last and looked back suspiciously. Danny sensed that it was fed up with his nonsense. He was afraid that it might suddenly come forward and peck at him with its strong beak or kick out with its powerful legs. He decided to retreat.

At the same time he heard his mother ringing the gong in the back garden, calling him to come home. It was really the wheel rim of an old plough hanging from the branch of a tree by a bit of wire, but when she struck it with a metal bar it made a tremendous din that rose up into the clear air and echoed away over the hillsides. 'Danny,' she called, beating the gong rapidly. 'D-a-n-n-y.'

He turned and started to run home down the slope, dodging logs, leaping over washaways, swerving past boulders and rocky outcrops until he came down onto the flat land near the house. There was a rickety mailbox near the gate with PATERSON printed unevenly on it. The backyard was a jumble of coops and fowlyards, woodheaps and dog kennels, fruit trees and compost heaps.

Beyond it were the paddocks of their little farm, with a few cattle, sheep and goats grazing in the late afternoon sunlight.

The farm was on the outskirts of the town. There were only a few hundred people in the place altogether — a main street, a few shops and offices, a service station, two churches, a hotel, a branch library, a school, and two bridges over the river. The houses were scattered about, sometimes in a broken row as if trying hard to line up into a real street, sometimes dotted further off with vacant blocks or clumps of trees between them.

The river started in the hills and ran down past the town. In summer it was nothing but a weary trickle with a few wide pools here and there, but after heavy rain it sometimes surged down in high flood and lapped the decks of the bridges with muddy water and brown foam.

As Danny came running into the back-yard his father was splitting wood for the kitchen stove. He glanced up briefly. 'Here, Danny,' he called. 'Take some of this in to your mother.' They both collected an armful and made for the kitchen. The sun was dipping down behind the hills and long shadows had fallen across the valley. It was suddenly cool, even cold.

'There'll be a nip in the air tonight,' his father said. 'Could be a frost in the morning.'

Danny was grateful for the warmth of the kitchen as they sat down to tea.

'What have you been doing today?' his mother asked. 'Exploring again?'

'I saw an emu,' Danny answered. 'A big one.'

'Really? In the scrub?'

'Yes. And it didn't run away. It just looked at me.'

His father was slicing the bread. 'They

12

often come down this way,' he said, 'heading for the river to have a drink.'

'D'you think there are more of them?' Danny asked.

'Sure to be. They usually move in groups — three or four together. Sometimes there are as many as a dozen or more.'

'I'll watch out for them,' Danny said. 'I like emus.'

2

Rescuing the Egg

The following day was the last day of the school holidays. Danny, and his best friend Billy Dunlop, were fishing for yabbies in a big pool beyond the west bridge.

Danny was almost twelve. He was well built for his age, nuggetty and strong, with fair hair and blue-grey eyes. Billy was only a few weeks younger but he was much smaller, with a freckled face and legs that were inclined to be bandy.

They had caught three or four yabbies and Danny was doing his best to coax another one forward so that Billy could slip his dab net under it from behind. They were using a chicken drumstick as bait. It was tied to the end of a long piece of string and Danny was tense with concentration as he eased it forwards very slowly with the yabby still clinging to it.

'Hey, Billy,' he called softly, keeping his eyes steadfastly on the line. 'Quick, get the net.'

Billy looked up. 'Ooh, what a beauty,' he said. With the net in his hand he stepped carefully into the water at the edge of the pool. He had to avoid stirring up mud or sudden ripples.

'Easy, easy,' Danny whispered.

Billy reached over and began to lower the net stealthily behind the yabby. But at that moment, just as they seemed certain to make the catch, chaos broke out all around them. A hail of clods and mud bombs rained down on the water in front of their faces. One hit Danny on the shoulder and another splattered across Billy's back.

'Surprise, surprise!' yelled a voice, followed by shrieks of laughter. It was Hacker Belton and his gang. His real name was Frank but nobody ever called him that, except Mr Moss, their teacher at school. Hacker was a yob who seemed to spend much of his time making life miserable for other people. He was older than everyone else at school and he was big — fat in the face and fat in the stomach. He always had four or five cronies tagging along behind him, not because they liked his company but because they were scared to break away from his gang.

Danny, who had been crouching at the water's edge, sprang up hastily to escape from the shower of mud, trod in a hole on the bank, and fell over on his back. Billy stood in the water, sheltering his head with his arms. Danny got up angrily. 'Ah, quit it will you?' he yelled.

The members of the gang were searching for more mud, pressing it feverishly between their hands and working it into small cannonballs.

'Out of the way,' Hacker yelled at Darren Wolfe, one of his hangers-on, at the same time shoving him aside so violently that Darren went sprawling into the water. He came up spluttering, then rushed at Hacker who was just preparing to hurl another shower of missiles at Danny and Billy. Hacker was bowled over by the onrush and as he fell Darren's foot came down hard in a tacky patch right in front of Hacker's nose. A spurt of black mud shot forward into Hacker's face.

'Ah, poo!' he yelled, spitting and wiping his mouth. 'I'll get you, Wolfe.' An instant later there was a free-for-all with everyone in the gang throwing mud at everyone else, pushing and wrestling one another, sometimes in the water and sometimes out of it.

Danny was disgusted. 'Come on,' he said to Billy. 'Let's get out of here.'

Billy picked up the gear. 'Where to?'

'Dunno. Anywhere would be better than this place with Hacker and his mob.'

'Why don't we go further up the river?'

'You can if you like.'

'Don't you want to?'

Danny shook his head.

'What are you going to do then?' Billy asked.

'Head for the hills I reckon. D'you want to come?'

Billy wasn't enthusiastic. 'Nah. Too much walking.'

So they parted. A few minutes later Billy was settling down at another pool and Danny was on his way up the slopes above the town, making for the scrub where he had seen the emu the day before.

Danny was at home in the hills. It was so peaceful there that he could hear the leaves rustling and the water gurgling in one of the creeks that fed the river. Far off a crow gave out its melancholy caw and a magpie carolled briefly. Now and again a mynah piped a few quick notes, as sharp and clear as crystal.

Danny walked slowly with his hands in his pockets. He passed the spot where he had seen the emu the day before and headed deeper into the hills. He skirted a rocky knoll, climbed through a cleft between a couple of big boulders, and came out onto a small plateau that was partly covered with bushes and saplings. He was looking ahead, trying to make out what lay beyond a clearing in the distance, and it wasn't until he was well past the boulders that he glanced down at the ground at his feet. Then he gasped and checked himself. A big goanna was facing him angrily, its body held high on all four legs, its head raised, its tongue flickering menacingly.

Danny retreated a step or two and began to search about with his right hand for a stick or stump that he could use to defend himself, never once taking his eyes off the goanna. He could understand why it was angry. He had disturbed it in the middle of a feast — a nest of big eggs on the open ground beyond the rocks. The place was littered with freshly broken shells. A half-eaten egg lay under the goanna's upraised chin. Only one egg was still intact. It was very beautiful — smooth, oval-shaped and dark blue-green in colour, the size of a biggish Easter egg. Danny knew at once what it was, even though his eyes remained fixed on the goanna. It was an emu egg. Some time during the past few weeks a pair of emus must have made their nest here and laid the eggs, and now the goanna was destroying them all.

His hand closed on a thick stick about fifty centimetres long. He straightened up, eyeing the goanna tensely. 'Shoo!' he shouted. 'Clear off!' The goanna's tongue flickered more threateningly than ever but it didn't move. 'Go on,' Danny yelled, 'egg thief. Shove off.' Still no response. Danny raised the stick above his shoulder, took aim, and threw as hard as he could. It missed the goanna by a fraction, skidding past its body, throwing up a scatter of dust and leaves.

The goanna reacted furiously. It reared up on its front legs, thrusting its long neck forwards and opening its mouth aggressively. Danny could see its teeth and its long forked tongue. The inside lining of its jaws was almost red in colour as though inflamed by the goanna's anger.

'Shoo!' Danny shouted again. 'Go on, get.'

At last the goanna moved, not with a scuttling rush as Danny had often seen them do, but quite slowly and deliberately. There was something insolent, even arrogant, about its attitude as though it was daring Danny to try something else. It swaggered off, moving step by step on its powerful legs, trailing its long tail over the loose leaves behind it with a faint rustle. Then, taking its time, it crawled up the trunk of a dead tree and paused a couple of metres above the ground — its body curving round the trunk in a kind of spiral, its tapering head angled upward.

Danny edged forward cautiously towards the nest and seized the unbroken egg. It was soiled and tacky with egg yolk from the smashed shells around it. He wiped it against his shirt. Then, holding it in both hands, he turned and raced off down the slope towards the river again.

Billy was still sitting on the bank holding the yabby pole and dangling the bait in the water. Danny came up to him, panting hard. 'Hey, Billy,' he yelled when he was still ten metres away. 'Look what I've got.' He held up the egg to show it off.

Billy jumped up and peered. 'What is it?'

'An egg. An emu egg.'

'Gosh, where did you find it?'

'In the scrub. There were a lot of them — a whole nest full — but a goanna got the rest.'

'What are you going to do with it?'

'Hatch it. Get a little emu out of it.'

Billy's eyes widened. 'D'you reckon you can?'

'Sure. Just have to keep it warm all the time.'

'How long will it take?'

'Don't know. But I'll find out.'

Billy moved closer. 'It's big, isn't it.' He held out his hand. 'Let's have a feel of it.'

Danny passed the egg over but just as Billy was about to take it another hand darted in from behind and snatched it away. It was Hacker Belton, who had come silently with his gang. 'Look what I've got,' he crowed, holding the egg up high and turning to the others. 'Let's have a game of keep-the-egg-away.' And with that he tossed it at Darren Wolfe who juggled it uncertainly for a second before finally catching it.

Danny rushed frantically at Darren.

'Give it back,' he yelled. 'It's mine. It's mine.' But Hacker and his group ignored his cries and started throwing the egg recklessly from one person to another.

3

Danny's Dream

The next few minutes were the worst in Danny's life. He dashed about madly trying to intercept the egg as it was thrown from person to person, but he always arrived too late. The egg travelled in hasty loops from Darren Wolfe to Kanga Kennedy, then to

Sylvia Leech and Tracy Gordon, on to Nong Whitehead, and finally back to Hacker Belton.

'Give it back!' Danny shouted. 'Give it back. It's mine.' But he might as well have shouted at the fenceposts by the river. Nobody took the slightest notice of him. There was no point in hoping that someone would take pity on him and hand the egg back. He knew that more than anything else they wanted to see him break down and start blubbering like a little kid. It was the sort of teasing torture that Hacker enjoyed.

It wasn't until Hacker tossed the egg to Darren for the third time that Danny had his chance. With a sudden lunge he pushed Darren aside while the egg was still in the air and then, turning quickly, he just managed to catch it before it fell to the ground. He started to sprint off with it but Hacker flung himself forward in a flying tackle and caught him by the legs. Danny came down in the sand on his knees and elbows but he still held on desperately to the egg. Before Hacker or any of the others could rob him of it again he threw it over to Billy who was standing uncertainly two or three metres away.

'Run,' Danny gasped. 'Go for your life.'

Billy caught the egg, spun round, and took off like a startled hare. He was a fast runner and he had a good start. Danny was confident that nobody would catch him. As it turned out, nobody tried. Danny stood up in a flash and gave Hacker a hefty shove just as he was getting to his feet. The bully went sprawling into the water and the rest of the gang pointed at him, hooting with laughter. Hacker blamed Nong Whitehead and came out, roaring revenge.

Danny saw his chance and dashed off after Billy. After a while Billy looked back and slowed down until Danny caught up with him. They were both panting and wheezing.

'Real creeps,' Danny said, 'Hacker and his mob.'

Billy checked to make sure that they weren't being followed.

'Deadheads,' he agreed. He handed the egg back to Danny.

'Thanks,' Danny said. 'Thanks for helping.'

'That's okay.'

'They would have smashed it for sure.'

'Yeah.'

Shortly afterwards they came to the crossroad that led off to Billy's place. 'Better be getting home,' Billy said, 'or Mum'll be hollerin'.'

Danny nodded. 'Me too.'

But when Danny finally hurried in through the kitchen door there was nobody home. He walked about from room to room for a minute, calling 'Mum', 'Dad', but there was no answer. He went back into the kitchen, looking about urgently for something to keep his egg in, but he couldn't see anything suitable. He put the egg down on the table and turned to search the dresser, but the egg started to roll towards the edge, gathering speed as it went. He saw it out of the corner of his eye and leaped back just in time, flinging out his arm like a cricketer fielding in slips. Miraculously the egg fell into his hand.

He blew through his lips in astonished relief. 'Phew.'

To make sure that such a thing wouldn't happen again he grabbed the woollen tea-cosy from the teapot and nestled the egg in it. Then he stood undecided. The tea-cosy was a good idea, not only because it stopped the egg from rolling about but because it helped to keep it warm. The question was, would it keep the egg warm enough, especially on cold nights? Clearly, he had to find out much more about emus and the way they hatched their young.

A dream was beginning to form in Danny's head — a dream about a little emu, hatched out in the house and growing up in the yard as a friendly pet, staying of its own free will. Danny's imagination was racing but there was so much that he didn't know: how long emus took to hatch, how fast the chicks grew, what they ate, what dangers they faced from cats or hawks. A whole lot of things.

He took the egg and the tea-cosy into his bedroom, pummelled a thick cushion with his fist until he had made a deep dent in it, put the egg in the hollow, and covered it with the cosy. He eyed it uncertainly but for the moment that was the best he could do. He had to learn a great deal more and he had to do it quickly.

He hurried out into the kitchen and looked at the clock. A quarter to five. If he sprinted he might just have time to get to the library before it closed. He raced out of the back door, dashed down the road over the bridge, and came panting up the main street with a couple of minutes to spare. Old Mrs Carter, the librarian, was sitting at her desk near the door. She looked up, partly surprised and partly annoyed, as he stumbled in noisily. Mrs Carter didn't believe in noise at any time, least of all in her library. She was grey-haired and as wrinkled as old leather. Her glasses always seemed to be on the verge of falling off the end of her nose. 'Sh-h-h-h,' she said as Danny clumped past, and then added in a whisper, 'Two minutes to closing time.'

Danny couldn't see the point of such elaborate silence, especially when the only other person in the library was Mr Limburger, a retired shopkeeper who lived by himself near the river. He was as bald as a rockmelon and his coat had leather patches on the elbows. He was reading the week's women's magazines. Although he had plenty of money he was too stingy to buy copies of his own.

Danny hurried across to the far corner, walking as gingerly as he could. He knew exactly where the books on birds and animals were kept and he was sure he had seen one there with an emu on the cover. It didn't take him long to find it. *The Life of the Emu* it said in bold print above a photograph of an adult bird and five beautiful little chicks. He sat down hastily at a table for a moment while he leafed through the pages to make sure that it had the right sort of information in it. Then he took it over to Mrs Carter and waited while she checked it out in his name. Neither of them spoke a word.

As Danny came out of the library he almost collided with Tracy Gordon. She had left the others and was on her way home. She was a lively girl with freckles on her nose and a crop of tousled honey-coloured hair. Danny got on well with her at school except when she was with Hacker's gang, and he knew that she only joined them because of her friend Sylvia Leech. 'Hi,' she said. 'What you got?'

He was cautious. 'Just a book.'

'About what?'

'Ah, nothin'.'

She craned forward. The picture on the front cover was plain to see. 'Emus?' She looked at him quizzically. 'You still got that egg? You goin' to try to hatch it?'

He blushed slightly. 'Try to.'

'Hope you do,' she said honestly. 'Be great if you could.'

He warmed to her. 'Yeah.'

'Where did you get it?'

'In the scrub. A goanna ate the rest.'

'Good thing the mob didn't smash it —
down by the river.' She seemed mildly
ashamed. 'Sometimes Hacker's a pain.'

He eyed her squarely. 'You can say that
again.'

He began to move off. 'See you.'

She gazed after him. 'Good luck then.'

When he arrived back home Danny
went straight to his room and started to read.
It was a wonderful book, full of details about
emus — their size, colour, food, nesting habits,
even the design of their feathers. He was still
engrossed in it when his mother called him to
tea. He sat down opposite his father who was
about to say, 'Well, what have you been up to
today, son?' as he usually did, but Danny was
too keyed up to wait for it.

'I found an egg, Dad,' he said. 'An emu
egg. A real beauty.'

His mother began serving up. 'That's
nice, Danny. Where did you put it?'

'In my room. I'm going to hatch it out.'

'Oh, do you think you can?'

'Sure. I'll have a little chick. An emu chick.'

'How are you going to hatch it? You couldn't put it under a broody hen. It would be too big.'

His father laughed. 'You certainly couldn't. The poor old hen would be perched up on it like a galah on a melon.'

'I'll keep it warm,' Danny said eagerly. 'I'll keep it warm in my room.'

'Don't be disappointed if it doesn't hatch.' His mother set Danny's plate in front of him. He looked down at it and recoiled. In the centre, surrounded by a mixture of vegetables, was a large fried egg, its yolk staring up at him accusingly like a big, unblinking eye.

4

Banished

After tea Danny said goodnight to his father and mother and went to bed early. But he didn't go to sleep. Instead, he sat up propped against a couple of pillows and went on reading the emu book. Beside him, on the floor, the egg was wrapped snugly in its tea-cosy, half-hidden among three or four cushions. Beyond it, Danny's radiator was standing near the chest of drawers, its red glow sending such a stream of steady heat towards him that even on the bed he could feel its warmth on his face and arms.

He read for a long time before finally dropping off to sleep. Because of that, and because of the unusual warmth in the room, he slept late the next morning. He woke up groggily to the sound of his mother's voice calling from the kitchen.

'You'll be late for school, Danny,' she shouted. 'Hurry up. Breakfast's ready.'

He ran to the bathroom, gave himself a dab and a splash, and dressed hastily.

'Five minutes,' his mother said. 'Quick, I've cut your lunch. It's in your schoolbag.'

He bolted down a bit of breakfast, grabbed the bag, and ran off down the road. The school bell rang just as he entered the yard. Billy came across to meet him. 'G'day. What happened — you're late.'

Danny grunted. 'Slept in.'

'How come?'

Danny was in no mood to explain his sleeping habits to anyone, not even Billy. He was no happier when Tracy Gordon called out 'Hi Danny, how's the egg?' as they jostled into the classroom. Too many people were getting to know about the egg. It was something he wanted to keep to himself.

In school he couldn't concentrate. All the facts he had been reading about emus kept going round and round in his mind. They tended to blot out the lesson on decimals that Mr Moss was trying to give. He had a half-finished example up on the blackboard.

'Now, six times eight,' he called loudly. 'What does that come to?'

A few hands went up. Nong Whitehead

twisted his face in painful effort and Darren Wolfe tried to look confident. Mr Moss ignored them both and picked on Hacker. 'Well, Frank?'

Hacker guessed. 'Fifty-four?' he asked hopefully.

Mr Moss was not impressed. 'Come on, come on,' he said, tossing a piece of chalk impatiently from one hand to the other. 'Six eights are …?' He paused while a few more hands went up. 'Yes, Tracy?'

'Forty-eight.'

'Right.' He wrote the figures on the board. 'Now, where do we put the decimal point?'

There was more silence, more intense mental effort. Suddenly he bent down and spoke directly into Danny's ear. 'Come on, Danny, where do we put it?'

Danny was far away on a saltbush plain in central Australia where five small emu chicks were pecking and pottering about in the wake of their parents. He came back to the classroom with a jolt. Mr Moss's question was still echoing in his ears but he had no idea where he was supposed to put some-thing, or what it was that he had to put there.

'Put … put what, sir?' he stammered.

There was a general hoot of laughter from the rest of the class. Mr Moss sighed, ruffled Danny's hair in good-humoured frus-tration, and went on to ask Peter Atkinson. For the moment he seemed willing to regard Danny's inattention as a normal case of Monday morning fuzzle-headedness.

Meanwhile, at home, Danny's mother was busy with a dozen household tasks. She had the sink full of sudsy dishes and the laundry basket full of damp clothes waiting to be pegged out on the line. There was a pungent smell in the air but she put it down to the combined effect of steam in the laundry and detergent in the sink. She rattled the breakfast cups, swished them with the dishmop, and stood them one by one on the rack to dry. She did the same with the plates and cutlery, drained the sink, wiped the table clean, and hung up the tea-towel.

The smell was very strong now — a smoky acrid smell as though something had become overheated and charred. She remembered the time when there had been a short circuit in the television set and some of the plastic-coated wires had melted. It was a smell like that. She went out into the laundry to pick up the clothes basket but paused at the door, sniffing suspiciously. There was certainly something nearby that was very hot. She glanced outside quickly to make sure that nobody was burning old tyres or rags in the paddock near the house and then went back inside. The smell was stronger than ever.

Convinced that something was wrong she hurried into the lounge to check the video, peered at the hot water service in the corner of the bathroom, and finally ran into her own bedroom to feel the electric blanket. Everything seemed normal. As she hastened back towards the kitchen she paused at the passage that led to Danny's room. The smell was very strong there. With a sudden pulse of fear she dashed up to Danny's door and flung it open. The sight made her reel. The room was thick with smoke and little tongues of fire were flickering along the edges of the cushion nearest to the radiator.

'My God!' she cried, leaping forward, hurling the burning cushion into the centre of the room, and trampling on it feverishly to put out the flames. Then she rushed to switch off the radiator, carried what was left of the half-burnt cushion outside, and returned to clean up.

Danny's egg was still in its tea-cosy. It had been sheltered by two or three other cushions and appeared to be unharmed. She picked it up and put it on the bed. 'Danny,' she said under her breath. It was an outrush of anger and relief and exasperation. 'Danny. That blasted egg.'

There was a scene at the tea table that night. 'You are not keeping that egg in your room,' his mother said. She was still a little white and shaken. 'Just think what would have happened if I hadn't been home today. You would have burnt the house down.' She was almost in tears.

Danny's father was stern. 'Your mother's right, Danny. You can't keep it in your room.'

Danny started to protest. 'But, Dad …'

His father set his mouth in a firm line.
'Danny, the egg goes.' Danny sat stubbornly,
looking down at his plate and saying nothing.
Suddenly his father pushed back his chair
and got to his feet. 'Right,' he said. 'That's it.'

Danny knew very well that his father
wasn't bluffing. 'I'll get it,' he yelled, leaping
ahead of his father. 'I'll put it in the cubby.'

His father paused threateningly. 'Okay,'
he said. 'And that's where it stays.'

It was a good cubby, tucked into a
corner of the backyard some distance from
the house. Danny had made most of it himself out of an old iron tank cut in half. It had
a kind of tunnel like the entrance to an
Eskimo's igloo leading up to it. He had put in
a floor of dry boards and a cupboard made of
boxes. There were cushions and an old car
seat to sit on. Two faded curtains hung across
the entrance to form a doorway.

Danny took the egg, still lying in its tea-cosy, picked up his big six-cell torch, and went out to the cubby. Once inside, he tried to heap as many warm things around the egg as he could — another cushion, part of an old woollen dressing-gown, one of his father's scarves, and an ancient jumper. Even then he was unsure. The sky was clear and frosty, and the cubby would be bitterly cold later in the night. If a little emu chick was indeed growing inside the egg Danny was doubtful whether it could survive a night like this. Looking at the egg in its pile of old clothes he suddenly made up his mind. The egg would be kept warm, no matter what.

He went back into the house and finished his tea. Shortly afterwards he said goodnight. In his room he pulled a beanie down over his ears, put on two pairs of thick pyjamas and woollen socks, and took the eiderdown from his bed. Very cautiously he let himself out through the window and made for the cubby. He knew it was going to be a long, cold ordeal so he wrapped himself up as thoroughly as he could in the eiderdown. Then he took the emu egg, still in its cosy, and put it inside his pyjamas. If grown-up emus were not available to keep the egg warm with the heat of their bodies, then Danny Paterson would do it instead.

5

Another Way

At school the next day Danny was out of sorts. His throat was sore and his voice croaked. Worse than that, he was beginning to realise that he couldn't possibly spend every night out in the cubby for the next month or two. It was quite out of the question. He wouldn't be able to bear the cold, and if his mother and father discovered what he was doing they would forbid it anyway. And they would never allow him to bring the egg back into the house. That was the real dilemma. He had to find some other way of keeping it warm — out in the cubby.

He was so preoccupied with all these thoughts as they kept floundering about in his mind that he was barely aware of what was going on around him. In actual fact everyone was practising 'The Lime Juice Tub', a good rousing bush song that they were going to perform in front of all the parents at the school's Open Day in three or four weeks' time. It had a catchy tune that had been a great favourite of the shearers of the district in times gone by:

When shearing comes lay down your
    drums,
Step on board, you brand new chums,

With a rah-dum rah-dum rub-a-dub-
*   dub*
We'll send you home in a lime juice
*   tub;*
We'll send you home in a lime juice
*   tub.*
We're shearing sheep in New South
*   Wales,*
Sheep that are as big as whales,
With leather necks and dirty tails,
And fleece as tough as rusty nails;
And fleece as tough as rusty nails ...

Mr Moss was very keen that they should put on a good show so he had gathered together a great array of bush band instruments as well as some good violins, flutes and recorders. Now he was beating time with his hands and watching carefully to make sure that all sections of his weird orchestra were playing their part. Danny and Billy were in charge of two sets of brass cymbals that had to be clashed together spectacularly at the right moments.

They were in the middle of their rehearsal, with Nong Whitehead bowing vigorously on the strings of his makeshift double bass and Darren Wolfe shaking the floor with thunderous thumps that were supposed to take the place of drumbeats, when Mr Moss suddenly raised his hand and the whole orchestra fell away into silence. He looked at Danny who was gazing vaguely into space. The cymbals were hanging idly in his hands.

'Come on, Danny,' Mr Moss said. 'What's the matter?'

Danny came back to reality with a shock. 'I ... I feel sick,' he said.

There were little jeering catcalls from Hacker and his mates but Mr Moss silenced them sternly. 'You feel sick?'

'Yes sir.'

He stood up and waved Danny to the door. 'All right. Outside.' Then he followed and shut the door behind him. On the porch he felt Danny's forehead and eyed him kindly. 'Is your mother at home today?' he asked.

'Yes sir.'

Mr Moss considered him for a moment and then seemed to make up his mind. 'Okay, I think you'd better go home for the rest of the day.'

'Yes sir.'

Danny picked up his bag and hesitated until the door closed behind Mr Moss. Then he jumped off the verandah and sprinted for home. As he came up the track towards the house he slowed down and tried to look especially miserable in case his mother saw him. He opened the screen door and stepped into the kitchen. 'Mum?' he called tentatively.

'You there, Mum?' There was no answer. He raised his voice and called again. 'Are you there, Mum?' Still no answer. Obviously his mother was out, probably doing a bit of shopping in the town.

A grin spread across Danny's face. He ran to the corner and dropped down on his knees in front of the cupboard near the sink. Hastily he pushed aside an assortment of basins and pie-dishes until he found what he was looking for — his mother's electric fry-pan. Lifting it out he carried it quickly to his cubby, fearful that his mother would come round the house at any minute and catch him.

Having done that he dashed back, seized the electric extension cord that his father kept hanging on a hook in the shed, and plugged it into the power point on the back verandah. Desperate for time he uncoiled it quickly, hiding as much of it as he could along the side of the house and in the grass beyond the clothes line. It was just long enough. He pulled the end through the entrance to the cubby and put it down near the frypan. Within a second or two he had connected it up and switched it on. Then he padded the inside of the pan with a woollen jumper and placed the egg in it. Success at last. He touched the metal under the jumper with his fingers to make sure that it was starting to warm up and sat back, eyeing it fondly.

A great sense of satisfaction swept over him. Now the egg could be kept snug and warm, and at a constant temperature, day and night.

He had only just finished in time. Suddenly old Blue, the Queensland heeler who lived in a kennel near the woodheap, started barking loudly — a happy welcoming bark rather than an angry warning one.

Danny guessed the reason. His mother was coming up the track on her way back from the town. Danny scuttled out of the cubby and raced round behind the fowlyard to make it look as if he had just come home. His mother saw him and stopped in surprise. 'Danny,' she exclaimed. 'Whatever are you doing here?'

Danny tried to look woebegone. 'I feel sick, Mum. The teacher sent me home.'

His mother was concerned. 'You poor boy.' She stepped forward and felt his forehead just as Mr Moss had done. 'You'd better come inside and lie down for a while.'

Sometimes it was nice to be treated as an invalid. Before long Danny was lying back on his bed with a glass of hot milk on the table beside him and the emu book in his hands. He had all the afternoon to finish reading it. Once or twice his mother popped her head round the door to see how he was getting on but then she went off to busy her-self in other parts of the house.

It wasn't until about three o'clock that a new and alarming thought entered his head as he was reading. His egg — or at least the tiny emu that he hoped was growing inside it — could be hurt by heat as much as by cold. It had almost happened with the radi-ator in his room. It could also happen with the frypan in the cubby.

Appalled at his own stupidity he jumped off the bed and raced outside, almost collid-ing with his mother at the back door.

'Danny,' she cried, 'whatever are you doing out of bed?'

'Won't be a minute, Mum,' he called. She was left speechless as he rushed out to the cubby and crawled through the entrance hastily on all fours like a running bear. Once inside, he seized the egg in its tea-cosy and quickly put it to one side. Then he pulled away the woollen jumper and the other pieces of cloth he had used as lining and touched the bottom of the frypan.

'Szzzz!' he exclaimed under his breath, snatching his hand away and flicking his fingers in pain. The metal was so hot that it had almost burnt his skin. He realised what an idiot he had been for not checking the setting on the thermostat before switching on the power. He hoped it wasn't too late. Seizing the control knob he turned it very deliberately from HIGH to LOW and waited to make sure that the base of the pan was beginning to cool down a little. He took the egg out of the tea-cosy and cradled it in his hands. It felt pleasantly warm but not hot. The thick woollen jumper seemed to have insulated it from the direct heat of the metal. 'Lucky,' he said to himself. 'Another few hours and the egg would have been cooked.'

Satisfied that all was well at last he packed the egg in its swaddling again and put it back carefully in the frypan, hoping that from now on there would be no more emergencies.

By evening he was feeling so much better that he said he would come out and have tea as usual in the kitchen with his father and mother.

'Been a bit off colour have you, son?' his father asked as they sat down.

Danny cleared his throat. 'A bit.'

'Better now?'

'Yeah, I think so.'

'He's been reading his emu book all the afternoon,' his mother said, 'so he can't be feeling too bad.'

His father smiled. 'And what have you found out?'

'All sorts of things,' Danny answered eagerly. He was so full of his subject that the details simply tumbled out. 'An emu hen can lay up to twenty eggs,' he said, 'and each one weighs almost a kilogram. It holds as much as a dozen hen's eggs.'

'Twenty at a time?' his father repeated. 'Really?'

'That's the limit. Mostly they lay eight or nine.'

'The mother bird must have a hard time keeping them all warm until they hatch.'

Danny's eyes were sparkling. 'But she doesn't do any of the hatching. She just lays the eggs and goes off. The father does all the work.'

'I might have known,' his father said with a smirk. 'Just like human beings.'

Danny's mother gave him a swipe with the kitchen mitten. 'Just the *reverse* of human beings,' she said, laughing.

'The father bird hatches the chicks and then he looks after them until they're grown up — sometimes for two years or more,' Danny added.

'And how long do the eggs take to hatch?'

'Eight or nine weeks — about sixty days.'

His mother smiled. 'Then you could be in for a long wait with *your* egg, Danny. Unless of course it was already a month gone when you saved it from the goanna.'

It was something Danny hadn't really thought about until now. 'I'll watch over it anyhow,' he said. 'No matter how long it takes.'

'Sure,' his father answered. 'There's nothing you can do except wait.'

6

Found Out!

After that everything seemed to run smoothly for a while. Even Hacker Belton behaved in a more civilised way for a change and the rest of the class were lively and friendly. Tracy Gordon asked Danny about the egg every day. She seemed really interested in what he was doing.

Billy, of course, came over to visit Danny after school, or on Saturdays, as often as he could. He was the only other person allowed to hold the egg. Sometimes he followed Danny into the cubby where he sat cross-legged on the floor while Danny reverently uncovered the egg, lifted it out of the frypan, and handed it over. Billy sat in awe, staring down at its beautiful shape and colour, feeling the smooth curve of the shell against his fingers. It was always pleasantly warm.

Although life was free of alarms for the moment, Danny was still preoccupied with thoughts about emus. He couldn't get them out of his mind, even when he was supposed to be concentrating on other things. Whether Mr Moss was talking about the forests of the Amazon at school, or the story of William Tell, or the diameter and circumference of a circle, emus would start walking across the picture Danny had in his head. They slipped in mysteriously, without warning, and stayed there for the whole lesson. Sometimes he sketched them in his book and coloured them in with brown and blue textas.

That was almost his undoing one morning when the class was having a spelling test. Mr Moss was walking about very deliberately, speaking in a loud voice as he made up sentences and emphasised the word he wanted them to spell. 'The travellers said it was the most beautiful sight they had ever seen,' he called. 'Spell *beautiful*.' And so it went on, word after word: *leisure, prophecy, alphabet, receive, accommodation, abattoirs, chasm* ... He was allowing plenty of time for them to write down the words and Danny found the pause between each sentence too long. He was in the process of colouring in an emu he had drawn on a piece of paper under his spelling pad, so he uncovered the drawing from time to time while he was waiting for the next word and went on with his emu. He wasn't even aware of the way Mr Moss was moving about the room.

Suddenly a shadow fell across his desk and he heard someone breathing above him. He desperately tried to hide his handiwork by thrusting his left arm forward but it was too late. Mr Moss's hand came down and pushed the sketch of the emu out into the open. Danny looked up guiltily and then hung his head, expecting some kind of axe to fall. To his surprise Mr Moss merely looked round the room and called the next word in a clear voice: 'The emu is an unusual creature. Spell *emu.*' Danny looked up fleetingly, just in time to catch Mr Moss's quick wink. It was wonderfully reassuring, and Danny felt a surge of happiness and gratitude. Not only was Mr Moss letting him off, but he was showing that he understood Danny's obsession. Perhaps he even agreed with it. The rest of the day passed quickly and happily — one of the best days Danny had had for a long time.

Meanwhile, back at home, his mother had been busy. She had spent the morning cleaning the house and airing the rooms. After that she had snatched a bit of lunch, baked a batch of biscuits, and decided to put a load of washing through the machine before Danny and his father came home. As soon as the bowl had stopped spinning she loaded the damp clothes into the clothes basket and hurried out to the line with it.

In her haste she dropped a tea-towel and a couple of pegs. As she bent to pick them up her eye glimpsed something in the grass nearby and she paused, still stooping, to see what it was. Even when she recognised it she was still puzzled. What was a cord, an electric cord, doing out here? It seemed to come out of nowhere and disappear into nowhere. Fascinated, she bent down and picked it up. Instantly she could see that it came from the power outlet near the laundry door, and ran off across the yard in the direction of the fowl shed.

She was suddenly filled with suspicion. Seizing the cord, she worked her way along it, hand over hand, like a sailor hauling in a rope. As she suspected, it led her straight to Danny's cubby.

When she reached the entrance she let the cord drop, got down on her hands and knees, and crawled inside. Ahead of her the frypan stood out clearly with its strange contents. She hurried forward, seized the whole bundle, and pulled the tea-cosy aside. She was left with the emu egg in her hands. At first she was rather grim-lipped — astonished rather than angry — but gradually she relaxed and a half-smile spread across her face. She tested the bottom of the pan with her fingers. It was beautifully warm, and so was the egg. The frypan was obviously doing its job.

She was still sitting there, wondering what to do, when there was a rush of running feet outside and the thud of a schoolbag being dumped. A moment later the curtains at the entrance to the cubby parted with a swish. It was Danny, home from school. He was in such a hurry that he had crawled right inside before he noticed his mother. Then he recoiled and stopped, frozen. For a second she thought he was going to turn and flee. He could see the egg in her hands and he knew that his secret was out.

'Danny,' she said firmly. 'You shouldn't have brought my frypan out here. You know that.'

He looked at her miserably and hung his head. 'I had to do it, Mum. I had to.'

'You should've asked, Danny.'

Danny was on the verge of tears. 'He would have died, Mum. The little emu would have died.'

She eyed him kindly, trying to think of the right words to say, but he went on with a rush. 'I had to keep him warm, Mum. I had to keep the egg warm. There was no other way except the frypan. And if we take it away now he'll die.' There was a catch in his voice. A sob rose in his throat.

She leaned forward and put her hand on his arm. 'All right, Danny, you can keep the frypan.'

'He'll die for sure,' Danny cried, trying to stop the tears that were gathering in his eyes. He was so overcome that he hadn't realised what she had just said. She inclined her head towards him and repeated her words just as her message dawned on him.

He checked himself, then impulsively put his arms round her neck and hugged her.

'Ah Mum,' he croaked. 'Ah gosh, Mum.'

She had trouble trying to see clearly. 'That's all right, Danny,' she said.

So they wrapped the egg in its cosy again, put it back in the frypan, and crawled out of the cubby together.

7

Tracy Helps

Now the world was a happy place. Danny was so keyed up over the frypan arrangement with his mother that his exuberance over-flowed at school. The following day, during the rehearsal of 'The Lime Juice Tub', he and Billy clashed their pairs of cymbals so deafeningly that Mr Moss looked up in surprise. After a while they not only clashed their own but began bashing one another's with high sweeping movements, first left, then right. They were both grinning broadly. Mr Moss shook his head in resignation. He couldn't quite make out what was getting into Danny Paterson lately.

By now Danny was so convinced he was going to hatch out a little emu chick that he began talking about a home for it — a fenced-in yard with a hutch or small shed where it would be safe while it grew up. He refused to believe that anything could go wrong — that the egg might be infertile, or that the baby chick might already be dead in the shell, or that a hawk or cat might seize it after it had hatched.

The following Saturday, therefore, he and Billy started work on the yard. First they gathered about a dozen narrow round posts

— some from the woodheap and some from the scrub — and assembled them near the fowlyard.

'If we build it here he'll be able to see the chooks during the day,' Danny said. 'They'll be company for him.'

Billy agreed. 'Yeah. And we can use the chook-house fence for one side of our yard. Save a lot of work.'

'Sure.'

When they had assembled the posts Danny brought the axe, mattock, crowbar and spade from the shed and marked out the boundaries of the emu yard. Then they started work. The posts were uneven in size but most of them were about one metre long and ten centimetres in diameter. By digging a shallow starting hole, sharpening one end of the posts with the axe, and then hammering each one into the ground as far as they could, they finally had a ragged line standing around the perimeter of the yard.

By then it was almost lunchtime. Danny had a blister at the base of his thumb, Billy had a black toenail because the crowbar had accidentally fallen on his foot, and both of them were ravenously hungry. They decided to head for the kitchen.

Just then Danny's father came by. 'Hullo,' he said goodnaturedly. 'What's all this?'

Danny made no secret of his plans. 'A yard for my emu.'

His father raised his eyebrows. 'A yard?'

'Yes. To keep him safe while he's little. Later on he can walk about where he likes — when he's big.'

His father tested one of the posts. It wobbled when he touched it.

'Some of them are still a bit loose,' Billy admitted.

Danny's father seized the crowbar, turned it upside down, and used the flat head as a stamper, plunging it into the earth around the base of the post. After half-a-dozen powerful strokes the post was as firm as a rock.

Danny tested it. 'Gee, thanks Dad. You can do the rest if you like.'

His father threw down the crowbar and smiled. 'After lunch, maybe. Time to go inside now. Your mother's waiting.'

All through lunch they chatted enthusiastically about emus and the emu yard.

'What are you going to use for the sides?' Danny's mother asked.

'Wire netting.'

'Where from?'

'There's a bit lying behind the woodshed.'

'That won't be enough.'

'And one side runs along the fowlyard fence.'

'Yes, but what about the rest?'

'I've thought of that,' Danny answered. 'There's a whole bundle of old stuff lying up in the scrub. Someone dumped it there in the bed of the creek.'

His father was sceptical. 'Is it still okay?'

'It's fairly rusty but it'll do. We'll pick the best bits.'

'Better take the cutters then.'

They set off after lunch, Danny carrying the cutters and Billy holding a long thin pole that they could hang the roll of netting on when they carried it back. It was a bigger job than they had expected. The netting, when they finally found it, was a tangled mess that had been dumped holus-bolus off the back of a truck. They had to straighten it and then cut out the best pieces bit by bit until they had a dozen scraps lying by the side of the creek.

'We're going to have to do some patch-ing,' Billy said. 'It'll take us a whole day to join all this stuff together.'

They managed to collect the pieces into a lumpy sort of roll, slipped the pole through it, and set off down the range. As they reached the flat ground near the town they saw four or five bike riders coming along the main road near the river. They were riding slowly, doubling back and doing wheelies just to kill time.

Billy looked up and squinted in the afternoon sunlight. 'Oh no,' he said. 'Don't say it's Hacker and his mob again.'

Danny had recognised them too. 'Don't take any notice of them,' he said.

Unluckily, Hacker took notice of Billy and Danny. He came riding up just as they reached the fence by the road and watched them from his bike. His followers did the same.

'What you got, Paterson?' he called. 'Chicken wire?'

'No,' Billy answered sarcastically. 'It's a boofhead trap.'

Nong Whitehead laughed and Hacker turned on him savagely. 'Shut up, will ya.'

Danny and Billy threw the roll of netting over the fence and started to climb through. But before they could pick it up again Hacker had jumped from his bike and seized it. He tore away several sections and ran off down the road with them, dragging them behind him in the dust.

Danny struggled through the strands of the fence and shouted after him. 'Bring that back, Belton.'

Hacker stopped and jeered. He held up the netting in front of his face and poked out his tongue. 'I'm going to make a monkey cage with this, Paterson, and I'm going to keep you in it.'

Darren Wolfe and Kanga Kennedy, who were in the group as usual with Sylvia Leech and Tracy Gordon, went to pull some more pieces from the roll but Danny rushed ahead of them, seized the carrying pole, and faced them angrily with it. 'Back off,' he shouted, 'or I'll clout you over the ears with this.'

They hesitated uncertainly and then retreated, but Hacker continued to gloat further down the road. 'D'you want your rotten netting back, Paterson? I'll sell it to you for a dollar.'

Danny was tense with anger and frustration. 'Bring it back here,' he yelled.

'One dollar,' Hacker called mockingly. 'That's cheap.' He paused. 'What do you want it for anyway?'

Sylvia Leech had sharp wits. She had already guessed the answer. 'For his emu,' she called, giggling and waving. 'For when it hatches out of the egg.'

Hacker hooted with derision. 'Emu?

Don't tell me you've still got that crummy egg, Paterson. I'll bet it stinks by now.'

Danny didn't know what to do. He and Billy were no match for the whole gang. If the two of them set off after Hacker and his mates they would probably lead them on a humiliating chase right into the town. Yet Danny was not the sort of boy who gave in easily.

It was Tracy Gordon who suddenly came to the rescue.

'Come on, Hacker,' she called, 'this is boring. And it's none of our business anyway.'

He turned on her. 'Ah, why don't you shut your trap, Gordon?'

Tracy's temper began to rise. She grabbed Hacker's bike which he had left lying by the fence and went off down the road with it, holding it with one hand while she rode her own bike with the other. 'I'll take your bike home for you,' she called cheekily, 'because you wouldn't be able to carry the netting on it anyway.'

'Hey!' he yelled in alarm, dropping everything and racing off after her. 'Give us back me bitser.'

Sylvia set off after them, shrieking with laughter. After a moment's hesitation Nong and Darren followed. Danny and Billy ran to retrieve the netting and then set off hastily for home.

'Hacker's nothing but a turd,' Billy said. 'A real bully.'

Danny looked back up the road where Hacker's group was dwindling in the distance. 'One of these days,' he said solemnly, 'I'm going to give Hacker Belton a thick ear.'

8

Goanna Attack

Danny was very grateful to Tracy Gordon for the clever way she had decoyed Hacker away from the wire netting. At school a few mornings later he thanked her in a bumble-footed way.

'Thanks, Trace,' he said, 'for ... er ... you know ...'

She paused and looked at him with bright clear eyes. 'For what?'

'For Saturday arvo. For what you did … you know … to get Hacker away.'

She smiled. 'Oh, that? It was nothing. Hacker's a pain anyway.'

'He sure is.'

Danny was more certain than ever that Tracy was about to break away from Hacker's gang, especially if she could persuade Sylvia Leech to do the same.

Unfortunately some of the other boys in the gang were almost as objectionable as Hacker, but in a different way. Darren Wolfe kept telling Danny that the egg was addled and would never hatch. He was a smooth talker. It wasn't until he showed Danny some examples of what he called 'emu-egg art' — eggs used for kitschy drawings and designs and tourist gimmicks — that Danny suddenly realised what he was up to. He wanted the egg for his own museum collection. That was clear enough when he offered Danny money for it. 'I'll give you two dollars,' he said, 'just to take it off your hands.'

Danny was horrified. 'Get lost,' he answered angrily.

'Three dollars.'

'Out of my way,' Danny shouted, pushing past Darren. 'I wouldn't sell it to you for a hundred dollars, not when I know what you want to do with it.' He paused, flushed and upset. 'There's a little emu in there, and I'm going to hatch it out.'

A few days later Danny ran into real trouble with Mr Moss. There were a number of reasons for it. Partly it was a case of plain high spirits because everything was going so well with the egg and the emu yard, partly because his dislike of Hacker still rankled after their clash at the weekend.

The band was rehearsing 'The Lime

Juice Tub' again and everyone was concentrating more than usual. The school Open Day was only a couple of weeks off now and a sense of urgency was beginning to creep into all the preparations for it: the items by the choir and the band, the exhibits of school work by every person, the class projects, library displays, mobiles, the indoor pet and nature study show, and the arrangements for folk dancing and afternoon tea.

Mr Moss had switched Danny from the cymbals to the gong because Swampy Waterman, the usual gonger, was absent. The gong had to be struck with a kettledrum stick that had a pad about the size of a golf ball on the end of it. Danny enjoyed his new role. Whenever his turn came he brought the stick down thunderously, then held it up ready for the next assault. The din was loud enough to vibrate everyone else's ears and rattle their eyeballs. Some of the other members of the orchestra looked up and grinned before bending to their instruments again.

Unfortunately for Danny he had only a few such moments of glory in the whole piece. The rest of the time he was unemployed. Hacker Belton was sitting nearby, playing the triangle, a mere tinkle of sound compared with Danny's gong. But the tinkle had to come much more often so Hacker was busy most of the time. It was a perfect situation for Danny to get some of his own back. He glanced round fleetingly to make sure that Mr Moss wasn't looking in his direction, then leaned over swiftly and gave Hacker a resounding thump on the head with the drumstick.

Hacker reacted predictably. He swung round looking for the culprit, at the same time putting up his right hand to feel the hurt above his ear. The triangle fell silent but Mr Moss was so busy watching other parts of the orchestra that for the moment he didn't seem to notice. Danny stared out of the window with an innocent expression on his face until Hacker turned to the front again. Billy, who had seen it all, grinned broadly.

Hacker resumed his tinkling on the triangle, and for a while everything went on normally until Danny seized the next opportunity and gave Hacker another thump. This time Hacker let out an angry cry. Mr Moss looked up sharply but as he didn't want to stop the piece in full flight he let it pass. If Danny had been satisfied to leave things at that everything would have been fine. He would have had his little revenge on Hacker and nobody but Billy would have been any the wiser. But he went on with it, thumping Hacker a third and finally a fourth time. The result was inevitable. Mr Moss, who was now lying in wait for it, looked up suddenly and caught Danny red-handed. He waved the orchestra to a stop and stood up.

'Right,' he said, pointing grimly. 'Outside.'

Danny tried to feign innocence. 'Who, me sir?'

Mr Moss wasn't one to be taken in. 'Yes, you Paterson. Out.'

And so it came about that at lunchtime Danny found himself on a special emu parade of his own, picking up every scrap of paper, orange peel, biscuit packet and greasy lunchwrap in the whole schoolyard. It was a job he detested. To make matters worse Hacker Belton and his followers sat in a group and jeered at him as he worked. As soon as he had finished cleaning up an area they tossed more wrappers and bits of litter on it behind his back. The last straw came when Hacker threw an empty coke can across the grass and hit Danny on the leg with it.

Instead of tossing it into the bin Danny seized it, spun round angrily, and hurled it

back at Hacker. It missed its target and skidded off across the yard, coming to rest at Mr
Moss's feet just as he came round the corner
of the building. He hadn't seen what Hacker
had done, and he didn't know that Hacker
and his gang had been needling Danny all
through the lunch hour.

'Paterson,' he called sternly. 'Pick that
up.'

Danny hesitated for a second, wondering whether he should try to justify himself,
but clearly Mr Moss was in no mood for it.
'Pick it up,' he repeated. 'And don't let me
catch you throwing things at other people
again. It's dangerous. And you know that it's
against the school rules.'

Danny went off sulkily. He felt a strong
sense of injustice. Hacker had been throwing
things too but he had got away with it. Now
he was sniggering and gloating, as he continued to do for the rest of the afternoon.

Danny's anger was still smouldering when he finally mooched off home after school.

He walked up the track from the main road, swung off to the left, and took a short cut past the fowlyard. It was the route he usually followed because it brought him right past the entrance to the cubby. The first thing he always did was to crawl inside to check the warmth of the emu egg. After that he usually walked quickly along the back verandah, pushed open the kitchen door, threw his bag in the corner, and went searching for biscuits or a piece of cake.

He was just passing the fowlyard gate, thinking vengeful thoughts about Hacker Belton, when he suddenly froze in his tracks. Out of the corner of his eye he had glimpsed something that set alarm bells ringing in his mind. It was a goanna, a big one, feasting on a nest of hens' eggs in the corner of the yard.

It had pushed its nose and shoulders

through a hole in the wire netting and was devouring egg after egg. Its broad scaly back, strong hindquarters and tapering tail lay on the outside of the fence. Danny could see every detail of its rough hide. It was even bigger than the one he had confronted up in the scrub when he had rescued the emu egg, and it was right here in his own backyard, not more than ten metres from the entrance to the cubby.

Danny went on the attack at once. He seized an empty feed bucket that was standing nearby and, without taking aim, hurled it blindly at the goanna. It was a lucky throw. The bucket made a fearful din as it struck the ground, skidded over the goanna's back, and crashed into a post near the corner of the yard. 'Get out!' he shouted.

The goanna was taken by surprise. It reared back out of the hole in the netting and then took off towards the woodheap at high speed. Danny watched it, standing angrily with a stick in his hand until it had disappeared behind the shed. He was outraged. If the goanna was bold enough to come right up to the house then nothing in the backyard was safe. Not even his emu egg. With a pulse of fear he turned and raced towards the entrance of the cubby.

9

Hacker Strikes

Danny swept aside the curtains with one
hand and crawled forward desperately. As he
reached the frypan he cast aside the woollen
covers and seized the tea-cosy. The emu egg
inside it was still intact.

He sat back, holding it in both hands

and breathing heavily with relief. For the moment the egg was safe. The longer he sat there, however, the more worried he became. A big goanna like that, roaming about in the yard, could sniff out his egg at any time. His father was at work all day, his mother was often away shopping or helping the neighbours, and he was at school. Who would prevent the goanna from crawling into the cubby?

It was plain that he could no longer leave the egg unguarded during the day when the goanna was out hunting. It was much too vulnerable. But what was the alternative? There was no safe place anywhere in the yard, and he had been forbidden from keeping the egg in the house. There was really only one solution — he would have to take the egg with him to school, either wrapping it warmly in his bag or carrying it against his body inside his jumper.

For a week or so everything went well. Billy was the only person who knew his secret. Even Tracy Gordon, though she asked about the egg almost every day, still thought it was being hatched back in Danny's house. Hacker Belton kept ridiculing Danny and called him 'Rotten-egg Paterson', but luckily he was in the dark too. And so things went on until the fateful afternoon before Open Day.

It was a day of turmoil. Apart from rehearsals, everyone was involved in a last minute panic: arranging bookwork, touching up displays, moving furniture, balancing mobiles and cleaning classrooms. And after lunch they all had to go home and return with their exhibits for the pet and nature study show.

It was an incredible assortment of tame and wild creatures that was finally assembled in Danny's classroom ready for viewing by parents the following morning: two cockatoos on perches, a galah, some bowls of goldfish, tadpoles, a bantam, a goanna, cages full of canaries and budgies, a terrarium, a frillnecked lizard, kittens, white mice, doves, a python, and a dozen other odds and ends. Mr Moss was in the middle of a sea of cages and milling children, trying to bring some sort of order to the chaos.

'The cockatoos over here,' he shouted. 'All the small birds along the far wall; the goldfish, tadpoles and terrarium on the desks in the middle ...' He broke off for a second and strode over to Hacker Belton who was poking a stick through the mesh of the bantam's cage, trying to topple it from its perch. Without a word Mr Moss seized Hacker under the armpits and hauled him aside like a tailor's dummy. Hacker looked sheepish and walked away.

'The lizards and the goanna on the

benches over here,' Mr Moss called. 'The kittens in the corner, the white mice ...'

At that moment Danny did something that proved to be very foolish. He and Billy were printing labels to go on the exhibits when they found they needed another black texta. 'I've got one,' Danny said, and without thinking he ran over to the spot where he had hidden his bag near the cupboard so that the emu egg in it would be safe from accidents. To get the texta he had to lift the egg in its tea-cosy covering, put it down beside him for a moment, open his plastic pencil case, and then replace the egg and shut the bag. He was quite unaware that Hacker Belton had been watching him the whole time.

As soon as Danny had gone back to Billy, Hacker sidled up to the bag, unzipped it, pulled the tea-cosy from the egg, and shoved it down inside his shirt. Then he walked over to the far side of the room pretending to be helping with the arrangements. As soon as Mr Moss's back was turned he slipped the tea-cosy onto his head like a beanie and waved gloatingly to Danny.

'What d'you think of me cap, Paterson?' he called. 'Fits okay, don't you reckon?' Danny looked up aghast. His only thought was for the egg, and what Hacker might have done with it. With a cry of rage he sprang across the room and flung himself at Hacker, pummelling him with his fists, reaching up and trying to tear the tea-cosy from his head. The other members of the class scattered, leaving Hacker in retreat before Danny's onrush. 'Give it back,' Danny shouted. Mr Moss heard the commotion and leapt forward. With a thrust of his powerful arm he swept Danny aside. 'Paterson,' he roared. 'What do you think you're doing?' He gave Danny a shove towards the door. 'Out, out.'

'But sir …' Danny began.

'Outside.' Mr Moss wasn't prepared to listen. 'You've had your chance. Go and empty the bins into the incinerator — all of them.' He pointed at the door. 'Now.'

Danny was still inclined to argue but Mr Moss silenced him angrily. Danny ran towards the cupboard to get his bag but he was even prevented from doing that. 'Out, Paterson. I want every bin emptied before you go home.'

Danny ran outside. He was seething. Once again Hacker had been the cause of the trouble and once again he had got away scot-free. If Danny had known it, Hacker was about to do something even more monstrous. As everyone was finalising the last details of the nature study display Hacker sneaked over to Danny's bag, seized the egg from it, and walked over openly to Mr Moss with it. 'Where should I put my emu egg?' he asked with a look of utter innocence.

Mr Moss was almost exhausted. 'Oh, I don't mind, Frank. Just leave it somewhere safe.'

'Over here on the bench?'

'Yes, yes. Okay.'

Hacker couldn't hide his smirk as he put Danny's egg down beside the goanna's cage. Then, most malicious of all, he flicked open the catch on the door of the cage as he went past, leaving the door partly ajar. The goanna flickered its tongue and moved forward cautiously, nosing the opening.

Meanwhile Mr Moss decided to dismiss the class without bothering to call them to order. 'Okay, you can go now. Don't forget your things in the morning. I want you here early.'

They all started streaming out. A few stragglers, including Billy, were still fussing with labels or food bins, but Mr Moss hustled them on. 'All right,' he called. 'Time to go.

Come on Billy. Come on Tracy.' He was obviously in a hurry to lock up and escape. 'You can finish the rest in the morning.'

Nobody had seen what Hacker had done, and Mr Moss had forgotten all about Danny. As the last two boys filed out he shut the door after them and locked it. Then he climbed into his car and drove away.

At that time Danny still had several more bins to empty. Just as he upended one of them Hacker came riding along on his bike. He stopped a few metres away, balancing himself with his feet spread wide on either side. 'The goanna's goin' to get your rotten egg, Paterson,' he called. 'He's gonna eat it, Paterson. He's gonna eat it.'

By now Danny was in a cold fury. Burning with the injustice of it all, stung by Hacker's jibes, tortured by his own helplessness, he suddenly acted on impulse. Rushing at Hacker he catapulted him from his bike and hurled him on his back. Before Hacker could recover Danny leapt forward, bent over him, and struck him a stinging blow on the cheek. He had wanted to hit him on the chin, perhaps remembering in some vague way how boxers fought in the boxing ring, but the blow missed and struck Hacker just below the eye.

If Hacker had been able to get up there would almost certainly have been a brawl in the schoolyard, but just then Billy came dashing over, shouting at the top of his voice. 'Danny, Danny! Your egg's lying on the bench, and the goanna's out of his cage!'

Danny forgot everything else and raced over to the classroom. He seized the door handle, wrenching and rattling it desperately, but it was firmly locked. He ran along the verandah, testing each window in turn, but they were all locked too. Billy came up just then and they both peered anxiously through the glass. The egg was there on the bench clearly enough lying in a patch of sunshine within a metre of the goanna's cage — the door ajar, with the goanna's long tapered head peering out suspiciously at its new-found freedom.

10

Despair

Danny was beside himself. He knew that it was only a matter of time before the goanna found the egg and ate it. Soon there would be nothing left but an empty shell.

Ideas raced through his mind. The other teacher had gone home and there was no point in trying to find Mr Moss. He lived in an old farmhouse five or six kilometres out of the town, and he drove his car like a speedway driver. He was probably halfway home by now. In any case, it was unlikely that he would believe a yarn about Hacker Belton stealing an emu egg and then purposely arranging for a goanna to eat it. It would sound like the biggest cock-and-bull story ever invented.

Unable to get back into the classroom to rescue his egg Danny decided that his only hope was his father. It was just on knock-off time so he could be in the hotel having a drink with some of his friends. Danny sprinted off down the street, calling 'Dad, Dad,' even before he reached the hotel corner. He peered hastily through the windows as he ran past but it was hard to see anything in the gloom. He pushed open the front door and ran inside. 'Dad,' he called again. 'Dad.'

A few drinkers turned and looked at him disapprovingly. 'Dad?' Danny called for the last time, but already his voice was faltering in his throat. There was no sign of his father.

Danny retreated through the door, leapt out onto the footpath, and tore off up the street, almost cannoning into Mrs Carter on the way. Only a miraculous sideways leap by Danny prevented him from spread-eagling the town's only librarian.

'Danny Paterson,' she cried out angrily, 'you should watch …' But Danny was already halfway across the bridge, heading for home as fast as a racehorse. 'Mum,' he shouted as he came hurtling up to the kitchen door. 'Mum, you there, Mum?'

He wasn't sure what his mother would be able to do, but she was very good in emergencies — and this was an emergency. There was nobody in the kitchen so he ran through to the other rooms in the house, calling more and more urgently. 'Mum, Mum, where are you?'

No answer, no sound, no movement. His mother was out and he was alone. It was the silence that broke his spirit. A terrible feeling of helplessness and hopelessness swept him. It was as though a door had been slammed in his face. There was nobody he could turn to now, nobody who could act in time to save his egg and the little emu inside it. All his work, all his care during these past long weeks had been in vain. Tears gathered in his eyes. With a sob he ran into his own room, flung himself on his bed, and buried his face in his pillow.

How long he lay there in misery he never knew, but eventually he roused himself, wiped his eyes with the back of his hand,

and went out to the cubby. He didn't crawl inside. Its emptiness would only have heightened the emptiness in his heart. Instead he sat cross-legged at the entrance, gazing listlessly at the woodheap, the emu fence, the fowlyard. The shells from the eggs that the goanna had broken still lay in the nest in the corner, with two or three new-laid eggs beside them. Danny eyed them without interest.

Goannas. They were really at the heart of everything — all his earlier happiness, all his present misery. They, and Hacker Belton. Yet goannas weren't really nasty creatures like Hacker. They didn't hurt people and they only ate things when they were hungry. Matt Thompson, who had brought his pet goanna to school for the nature study show, said they were the gentlest creatures in the world as long as they were well fed. Matt's father owned a poultry farm so they fed their goanna on rejected and undersized eggs and bits of chicken. It was a real pet — so tame that it came up and ate out of their hands.

A vague idea suddenly stirred in Danny's head. It was Thompson's goanna that was in the schoolroom. Matt would have fed it well that morning so it wouldn't be hungry now. And if it wasn't hungry it wouldn't be interested in the emu egg — not yet. Perhaps there was still time to rescue it.

The broken shells and eggs in the fowl-yard caught his eye again. It was hard to avoid seeing them because they were lying right before his gaze. A glaze of yellow yolk had dried over some of the pieces, giving them a freshly smeared look, as if the goanna had only just finished feasting on them.

Danny suddenly stared hard at the shells and unbroken eggs. A new idea was beginning to form in his mind — a bold, cheeky idea. His eyes shone as it took shape, and a grin spread across his face. It was an incredible notion. Brilliant. And just a bit dangerous.

He leapt to his feet, grabbed a hessian sack from the shed, and set off across the paddock towards the hills. He looked up anxiously at the sun. Although it was low in the sky he knew that sunlight would still be streaming through the classroom window onto the desk where the egg was lying. The egg would still be warm, provided the goanna hadn't already eaten it. But when the sun set, everything would be in shadow. For a short time, perhaps an hour or so, the warmth of the room and the desk would keep the little chick alive, but after that the egg would get colder and colder and the chick would die. Danny knew he was racing against the clock.

He zig-zagged his way hastily across the face of the slope, toiled up the rocky knoll ahead of him, swung behind the two big boulders he knew so well, and finally came out on the flat scrubby ground where he had found the emu egg. The remnants of the nest were still there. He quickly gathered up the pieces of shell from the eggs the goanna had broken, handling the two or three best pieces very carefully, and put them in his bag. Then he turned and ran back home as fast as he could.

His father and mother were just coming up the road as he arrived, so he dashed to the fowlyard, grabbed a couple of hens' eggs, and put them in the bag too. Then he rummaged through his father's collection of tools in the woodshed and selected a strong pinch-bar with a curved claw-like blade at one end and a chisel edge at the other. He just had time to hide everything in his cubby before his parents came round the side of the house and stepped onto the back veran-dah.

'Hullo, Danny,' his mother said. 'Sorry we're a bit late.'

Danny tried to look unconcerned. 'That's okay.'

She started bustling about. 'Everything ready for the big day at school tomorrow?'

Danny was defensive. 'I guess.'

'I'll get tea ready. It'll only take a minute.'

His father took off his coat. 'Get your mother an armful of wood, would you, Danny?'

'Yes Dad.' Danny ran off, glad to get away. The last thing he wanted was a string of questions about the events of the day.

Danny gulped down his tea and then said goodnight. 'I think I'll go to bed early,' he said, trying to make it sound like a casual comment.

'Good idea,' his mother answered. 'You've got a big day tomorrow.'

But bed was the last thing in Danny's mind. After waiting breathlessly for a few minutes he seized his big flashlight, eased himself out through his bedroom window, gathered his gear from the cubby, and ran silently down the track towards the town. Keeping to the shadows near trees and buildings as much as he could he made his way stealthily up to the boundary of the school, scuttled across the yard, and crept noiselessly onto the verandah of his classroom. By now it was quite dark.

Here he was very much out in the open so he had to act quickly. He ran along the line of windows with his torch, testing each one for strength and firmness. The frames were old and the locks were loose. They rattled as he shook them. Unluckily he was concentrating so hard on what he was doing that he didn't see the empty bin standing in his path, exactly where he had dumped it earlier that afternoon. As he blundered into it unexpectedly it fell on its side, lost its lid, rolled off the edge of the verandah, and crashed down onto the asphalt surface of the playground with a shattering din. Danny almost swallowed his windpipe with fright. Quickly switching off the torch he crouched against the wall of the classroom, holding his breath.

At the sound of the bin, Ben Hooper's Alsatian went into a frenzy. The Hoopers lived just beyond the schoolyard. Suddenly their front door opened and the porch and garden were flooded with yellow light. Danny crouched motionless. Ben Hooper stood in the doorway for a moment and shouted angrily at the dog. 'Shut up, you mongrel.'

The dog stopped barking and trotted over to him. 'What's the matter with you,' Ben called, 'you big mutt? Settle down.' There was silence for a while and then Ben turned and went back inside. The light snapped off and the welcome darkness swallowed the place again.

Danny breathed more easily. He waited a little longer, then crept up to the centre window and wedged the end of the pinch-bar under the frame. The timber was warped and loose so the bar slid in easily. Gritting his teeth Danny bore down on the bar with all his strength. He needn't have tried so hard. There was a sharp click — whether it was the sound of the old swivel-lock actually break-ing, or whether he had just forced one part of it away from the other, he didn't know — and then the bottom half of the window slid open quietly.

Danny was jubilant. He lifted his hessian bag through the opening and climbed in after it. As he did so the headlights of a passing car slashed a bright blade of light across the wall outside. Danny had just made it in time. He stood up and shone his torch around the room until the beam rested on the bench near the goanna's cage. The cage was empty but Danny's egg was quite intact. With a feeling of intense joy he moved forward to retrieve it.

11

Danny Triumphant

The next morning Hacker Belton came to school early. The cheek under his right eye was rather puffy and the skin was dark. He rode straight up to the classroom on his bike and peered through the window. The emu egg was gone. In its place on the bench there was a cluster of shell fragments smeared with yolk and slippery blobs of egg white. Some of the mess had spread across the wooden surface of the bench, and one or two streaks had run down the wall.

Hacker pressed his nose against the glass to get a better view and grinned broadly. Then he pedalled over to the footpath and sat straddling his bike as the rest of the class began to arrive.

Danny and Billy finally came along together. They were both wearing jeans and thick jumpers, and Danny had a jacket over his shoulders as well. He held his left hand against his body as if he had a stomach ache. Nobody but Billy knew that the emu egg was snug and warm under all that clothing.

Hacker smirked as they drew level. 'Guess what the goanna's had for breakfast this morning, Paterson?' he called.

The boys ignored him and walked on.

'He must've enjoyed it,' Hacker called. 'Hardly left a scrap.'

Still no response.

'Your rotten old egg's busted, Paterson.'

Danny glanced at Billy and gave him a secret grin. Then, because Hacker could only see their backs, he gave his stomach a friendly pat as though reassuring the egg that all was well. Billy giggled and Hacker was crestfallen. He couldn't understand why his news had fallen flat. Danny should have been wailing and tearing his hair by now.

For Hacker there was still worse to come. When Mr Moss arrived and unlocked the room he was brisk and businesslike. Everything had to be shipshape, ready for the arrival of the parents and the beginning of the performances. As soon as he saw the mess on the bench he called Hacker over.

'Bad luck about your egg, Frank,' he said, 'but we can't have a mess like that in the room.' He grabbed a rag and thrust it into Hacker's hands. 'Here, take this and clean it up. Then get a bucket of soapy water and wash it down properly.'

Danny and Billy who were standing nearby laughed gleefully and then turned away in case Mr Moss became suspicious. But as soon as he was busy elsewhere they waved to Hacker, pointing at the eggshells and chortling with delight. Hacker was as mystified as he was furious. 'Ah, shove off,' he hissed. 'Go bag your heads.' It was the sweetest revenge Danny could ever have imagined.

By ten o'clock, when the items were due to begin, a great crowd of parents and visitors had gathered at the school. They were seated on forms and chairs arranged in a wide semi-circle on the asphalt in the yard, with the performing area in front of them. Every item earned loud applause — first some games played by the junior boys and girls, then folk dancing, gymnastics, a Maypole dance, and a bracket of songs from the choir.

It was a lovely morning, warm and sunny, with a few wisps of cloud and barely a breeze. Danny almost felt hot in his thick jumper but it was impossible for him to take it off. When Mr Moss finally announced 'The Lime Juice Tub' everyone in the band could see that he was slightly on edge. He glanced at them anxiously as they took their places with their instruments and beckoned the slow movers forward impatiently. It was obvious that he wanted to make a good impression. At last he held up his baton, waved it rhythmically to the beat of the tune, and whispered loudly 'One … two … three.'

Although the start was a little ragged they soon got into the swing of it and played with gusto. They realised that Mr Moss was on show too and they wanted to do their best for him. They finished the first stanza in great style and were just reaching the peak of their performance when Billy suddenly saw Danny double up in mid-swing and clutch his stomach as if recoiling from a stab of pain.

It lasted for only a second or two, and then Danny seemed to collect his wits and went on playing, looking rather guilty and hoping that nobody had noticed. Unfortunately they had played no more than a few bars when the same thing happened again. This time a good many people couldn't help being aware of it, including Mr Moss and Danny's mother and father. The agonised expression on Danny's face, and the sudden clutch at his stomach, suggested a spasm of intense pain. Mr Moss continued to beat time but he kept gazing at Danny anxiously.

When Danny clutched at himself for

the third time it was too much for his father and mother. They left their seats hastily and hurried round at the back of the audience and helped Danny down from the platform. They were both convinced that he was really ill. Mr Moss persevered valiantly but there was such a stir among the spectators and musicians alike that people were paying more attention to Danny than the perform-ance. In the end Mr Moss gave up in despair and waved his baton sharply to end the item.

Meanwhile a great revelation dawned on Danny. He quickly lifted up his shirt and jumper and took out the egg from its snug spot next to his skin. There was a hole in the smooth blue-green shell, and a strong little beak was protruding from it. Now and again it moved backwards and forwards in a peck-ing motion. Even as everyone watched there was a minor convulsion inside the egg, a big-ger piece of shell broke away, and a mottled head popped out to view the world. Danny's egg had hatched.

He caught a fleeting glimpse of Hacker Belton with a look of utter bewilderment on his face before Billy shouted, 'You've done it, Danny.'

It was such a breathtaking moment that Danny couldn't quite believe it himself. His eyes were wide and his mouth agape. 'I have too,' he said at last. 'I've done it. I've done it.'

It was the end of 'The Lime Juice Tub' but no one seemed to mind. The hatching of Danny's egg was a more astonishing perform-ance than any item on the school program. The news swept out into the town and spread through the district like wildfire. Even Mr Moss didn't mind because, as Danny's teacher, he somehow shared the glory of the moment.

As for Danny himself, he knew that his life would never be quite the same again.

12

Epilogue

A few months later there was a great celebration to mark the town's jubilee. It lasted for a week, with competitions, sports matches, the unveiling of plaques, family gatherings, sheep shearing contests and an old-time ball when everyone dressed up in period costumes. But the most spectacular event of all was the Grand Parade through the main street.

Everyone and everything, it seemed, took part in the parade: dozens of floats, ancient steam engines, brass bands, horses and wagons with ribbons tied to them, vintage cars, camels, an old fire engine, buggies, horsemen, old soldiers marching in their wartime uniforms, country fire officers with their modern equipment, a bullock wagon, and a group of local marching girls.

Large crowds of visitors from the surrounding districts flocked into the town to see the sights and stood three or four deep on both sides of the street, waving and cheering. One of the biggest cheers went up for a bright float that was made up of a bushland scene with models of kangaroos, wallabies, and other animals and native birds in it. Down both sides of the float a slogan had been printed in large letters for bystanders to see. HELP SAVE OUR WILDLIFE, it said. The float was pulled by a tractor driven by Danny's father, and sitting prominently on a seat at the front of the float were Danny Paterson and Billy Dunlop.

Danny was holding something that brought more cheers and shouts of approval and good humour from the watchers. It was really a living example of what the slogan on the float was all about — a live emu chick, cheeping and peeping happily in Danny's arms.